GROSSET & DUNLAP
An Imprint of Penguin Random House LLC, New York

Inspired by the original book retold by Watty Piper
with illustrations by George and Doris Hauman.

Visit us online at www.penguinrandomhouse.com.

ISBN 9780593094334

1 0 9 8 7 6 5 4 3 2

LOVE

from

The Little Engine That Could®

illustrated by Jill Howarth

Grosset & Dunlap

When I'm on my way . . .

. . . and I don't know where to go

. . . I know I can follow your lead.

Even when things look dark . . .

. . . and the hill is steep

♥

. . . you always give me
the push I need.

And if things get in the way,
or I get off track . . .

♥

... I know you've always got my back.

In the cold . . .

... or in the heat

. . . you make me . . . *me*!

♥

Together we can do anything.

That's why . . . I love you!